SWEET FORGIVENESS

Amish Romance

HANNAH MILLER

Tica House
Publishing

Sweet Romance that Delights and Enchants!

Personal Word from the Author

To My Dear Readers,

How exciting that you have chosen one of my books to read. Thank you! I am proud to now be part of the team of writers at Tica House Publishing who work joyfully to bring you stories of hope, faith, courage, and love.

Please feel free to contact me as I love to hear from my readers. I would like to personally invite you to sign up for updates and to become part of our **Exclusive Reader Club** —it's completely Free to join! Hope to see you there!

With love,

Hannah Miller

VISIT HERE to Join our Reader's Club and to Receive Tica House Updates:

https://amish.subscribemenow.com/

Chapter One

Guilt could make a man do things he'd swore he'd never do.

Jeremy Slagel had promised himself he'd never return to Baker's Corner, Indiana. Yet, here he was. And none too happy about it either.

He pulled open the door of the dry goods store, a cheery bell jingling in jarring contrast to his current mood. He stepped inside.

"Jeremy?" the shop owner greeted him in a loud voice, an expression of surprised recognition crossing his lined face. "It must be about five years since the last time I saw you in here. What brings you back to town?"

"I'm taking care of the family farm now that my *daed* has become too sick to handle the chores any longer."

Jacob gave Jeremy an approving nod. "It's *gut* that you're back."

Jeremy made a noncommittal sound in response. Unfortunately, he couldn't agree with the older man's sentiment. This was the very last place in the world he wanted to be.

Growing up, he couldn't wait to leave, and he'd hightailed it out of Baker's Corner at the first opportunity—the same way his four older brothers had left before him. Now he was back. The only one of the five Slagel boys who had felt compelled to return.

His conscience had a lot to answer for. Especially given the fact that his feelings for this place—and for one man in particular—were entirely justified.

He ignored the knowledge that not everything about Baker's Corner had been unbearable, but things had been bad enough. And that came down to just one reason—Jeremy's *daed*.

After all the misery he'd wrought throughout Jeremy's boyhood, Isaiah Slagel didn't deserve consideration from his youngest son now. But even knowing that, Jeremy hadn't been able to ignore the bishop's summons when he called Jeremy back home.

Nee, not home, he thought. This place wasn't home. Not anymore. It hadn't been for a long time. He lived in Illinois now. His life was there, and he intended to return to his farm just as soon as he was able.

Jeremy felt a sharp pang of shame at the relief the thought brought, since his eventual escape hinged on a man's death. His *daed's* death. After the older man was gone, Jeremy's duty here would be done.

He felt guilty for that thought, too.

Caring for a family member shouldn't be an unwanted obligation. But Isaiah Slagel had never been an easy man to love. Even his wife hadn't been willing to stick around, leaving her five young sons to be raised by the cold and dictatorial man after she fled the place.

Jeremy pushed away the painful thoughts of the past, refusing to dwell on them. Since coming back, he had enough to deal with in the present. Like struggling to find some way to get along with his *daed* when he'd never been able to do it before.

Jeremy feared that the best he could hope for was just to get through it.

He wished things could be different, but he'd learned a long time ago that Isaiah Slagel would never change. The older man had never asked anybody for anything—he gave orders and made demands, expecting everyone else to jump to attention and do his bidding without question.

Even on his deathbed, Isaiah was still ordering Jeremy around, unappreciative of his efforts to help, throwing them back in his face rather than giving Jeremy even a single word of thanks. This left Jeremy with a smoldering resentment he couldn't seem to rid himself of no matter how hard he tried. That, in turn, made him feel rotten that he couldn't find some sort of forgiveness in his heart for a dying old man.

Jeremy was tired of feeling guilty. But there was no denying the truth of his ugly emotions. At least, not to himself. And most certainly, not to *Gott*.

"What can I do for you today?" Jacob asked, breaking into Jeremy's silent self-recriminations.

"I need to stock up on several items," he replied as he withdrew a list from the waistband of his trousers.

Although he was in no hurry to return to the farm where his *daed* lived outside of town, delaying wouldn't change what was waiting for him. There were fields that needed to be plowed and animals to tend—and a surly patient who required Jeremy's help, though his *daed* would surely deny ever needing any sort of help from one of his sons right up to the moment he took his last breath.

Completing his purchases, Jeremy turned toward the door of the shop, but he pulled up short when his gaze landed on a young woman whose reddish-gold hair peeked from beneath her white *kapp*. He had no difficulty recognizing Lovina Wyse, despite the years that had passed.

She still had a smattering of golden freckles on her cheeks, and her features were the same. But the welcoming expression he used to see on her face was gone. Her slim frame was clothed in a dark navy dress that made her ivory skin stand out in sharp contrast. When her eyes met his, there seemed to be a distinctly wary look in their green depths. Though he had no idea what might have put it there. Or maybe he did. They had not parted under the best of circumstances.

He had felt more than a few regrets about saying goodbye to her—but not enough to make him stay. That didn't mean he hadn't missed her, though.

It had been almost five years since he'd last seen her, but he'd thought of her more often than he liked to admit. Memories of her had snuck up on him when he'd least expected them—recalling her sweet smile and the way her eyes sparkled when she was happy.

At the moment, her mouth was pressed into a thin line and her gaze was flat as it focused on him.

If he had crossed her mind at all in the intervening years, he doubted it had involved any fond memories.

She didn't say anything and neither did he. He didn't know what to say. They'd been friends once, but that had been long ago. He'd always known there could never be anything more than friendship between them, and he'd been at pains to ensure that no deeper feelings had a chance to develop. Even before he'd left town, a distance had grown between them.

Though it had been by his choice, that didn't make this first unexpected encounter any easier.

As they both stood motionless, an awkward silence stretched out between them until he finally broke it by clearing his throat. But Lovina spoke before he could get any words out.

"I'm surprised to see you here, since you made no secret of your desire to leave and never return."

He shifted from one foot to the other, his gaze dropping away from hers. "I never planned to come back—"

"So what changed?"

Nothing. His desire to leave this place was just as strong as it had always been. Maybe even greater since he had a life waiting for him somewhere else. Yet...he still found himself wanting to linger in Lovina's company.

Giving in to that urge would only lead to trouble, however, and he stuffed the urge down as far as he could inside him, wishing he could make it disappear completely.

"I'm just here for a short time to help out my *daed,*" he repeated what he'd already told himself at least a dozen times before.

Chapter Two

And then he would be gone again. Although Jeremy Slagel left those words unsaid, Lovina Wyse heard them loud and clear.

He was just as handsome as she remembered which caused a pain in her heart. Though she had tried to convince herself that her memories had built him up into more than he really was, that wasn't the case.

If anything, her memories faded in comparison to the man standing in front of her now. His square jaw seemed firmer, and his eyes were a more brilliant shade of blue. He wore his dark brown hair a bit longer than he once had, the wavy texture now more apparent than it had been when she'd known him before. He was dressed in dark trousers held up by suspenders, and his white shirt emphasized the deep tan on his face, evidence of the hours he spent outdoors.

The same restlessness she recalled from years ago when he'd been a boy still seemed to cling to the man. No doubt it was due to being forced to come back here.

It was apparent that he couldn't wait to return to the life he'd left behind in Illinois. And why not, when he'd made it plain that there would never be anything to keep him in Baker's Corner on a permanent basis. Not his *daed*, nor his family's farm. And certainly not Lovina.

Jeremy opened his mouth as though he intended to say something more, but then he closed it again without speaking. Lovina wondered what he was thinking but pushed her curiosity aside. She didn't want to care about the thoughts that filled his head. She couldn't afford to—not when he would soon be leaving again.

She *didn't* care about his thoughts, or the fact that he was eager to leave, she assured herself, lifting her chin. "Well, then, don't let me keep you. I have things to do, as well." She forced her voice to remain even and tried to hide her trembling.

He stared at her for a moment longer before giving her a brusque nod in parting, then he stepped around her without another word and exited the dry goods store. The bell on the door jangled as it closed behind him, and she couldn't stop herself from turning around to watch him through the front window of the store. He walked toward a dusty, black buggy parked on the street. After he loaded his supplies inside, he pulled himself up onto the padded bench seat and took up the reins, setting the horse in motion without a backward glance.

A moment later, he disappeared from sight, and Lovina released a heavy sigh.

She refused to acknowledge the emptiness she felt that he hadn't asked her how she was doing or hadn't shown even the slightest interest in what had been going on in her life since he'd left town. Of course, not much had changed for her. She was still helping her frail *mamm* and caring for her ailing *daed*. The older woman's arthritis had only gotten worse as the years passed, and she was unable to do much work around the house any longer.

Jeremy couldn't know that though, since she felt certain he hadn't kept up with all the happenings in Baker's Corner. He did know, however, that her parents' health had not been the best even five years ago. Yet, he hadn't even bothered to inquire as to how they were getting on.

Lovina would have hoped he would express a bit more concern and compassion given that his own *daed* was doing so poorly. But perhaps that explained why he hadn't acted in a more sociable manner. He was likely distracted by his own troubles.

Or maybe he simply has no interest in talking to me. As had seemed the case even before he moved away.

She shouldn't be hurt by his apparent indifference to her,

especially since it was nothing new. Surely, she should be used to it and not allow it to affect her.

They had been close once, despite the fact that he was a couple years older than she. But after he'd left school and started spending the majority of his time working on his family's farm, she hadn't seen much of him. It seemed a perfectly responsible explanation for the distance that had grown between them, yet she'd sensed there was more to it than he was admitting. That he was using the work on the farm as an excuse.

And it had hurt her more deeply than she liked to admit.

They had rarely talked after that and had drifted apart long before he left town. Though she would like to place the blame solely on him for that, she would be lying to herself if she didn't admit she had started acting a bit distant toward him when it felt as though he were deliberately rebuffing her attempts to continue their friendship. She hadn't understood his actions, and it had plagued her for a long time, like a sore tooth that wouldn't heal. Finally, she had forced herself to stop poking at the raw nerve.

Of course, none of that mattered now anyway. It was all in the past and there was no changing it, no matter how much she might have yearned for things to be different. She used to entertain silly, girlish hopes about Jeremy Slagel suddenly wanting to court her and one day asking her to marry him, but she had put those foolish dreams aside for good on the day he'd left Baker's Corner—and her—behind.

She didn't have time to waste wishing for what could never be. She had too much to do, working at her family's bakery and tending to things at the house where she lived with her parents. The task had fallen to her since she was the only one of her siblings without a family of her own. It just made sense that she would be the one to care for her *mamm* and *daed*. Of course, her older brothers and their wives did their part, running the family bakery so their parents still had an income. Because of that, Lovina didn't have to struggle to put food on the table or keep a roof over their heads—or to pay for remedies to treat their ailments.

Footsteps sounded on the hard wooden floor as the owner of the dry goods store approached her.

"It's nice to see Jeremy Slagel back in town again. Maybe, he'll decide to stay this time." The older man didn't give Lovina a chance to respond one way or the other before he continued. "What can I help you with today, Lovina?"

Although it took more effort than she would have liked, Lovina pushed all lingering thoughts of Jeremy from her mind and focused on the task at hand.

Chapter Three

"What took you so long?" Isaiah Slagel demanded the moment Jeremy set foot inside the farmhouse.

The words were hollered from the room on the first floor where a bed had been set up for the older man since the stairs had become too difficult for him to navigate. His health had gone downhill quickly after that, and now Isaiah couldn't even leave the bed—which left Jeremy at his *daed's* constant beck and call—or more accurately, at his bellow and command.

Annoyance flooded Jeremy as he nudged the front door closed behind him, his arms weighed down with the items he'd carried in from the buggy. He set down the heavy wooden box with a little more force than necessary, struggling to rein in his emotions. *Gott, give me patience*, he silently appealed heavenward.

"Well?" Isaiah shouted when Jeremy didn't respond quickly enough to suit him.

Jeremy's hands curled into fists at his sides. Not even a "*denki*" in thanks for making the trip to the dry goods store to purchase food for the older man before he'd started in on Jeremy again.

But then Jeremy knew better than to expect anything else. Though that did nothing to cool his temper.

Taking a deep breath to calm himself, he relaxed the tight grip of his hands and walked down the hallway. He paused in the doorway of his *daed's* room.

Heavy curtains were pulled across the windows, blocking out the midday sunshine. The only light in the room came from the lantern sitting next to a Bible on the bedside table, where the untouched breakfast that Jeremy cooked for Isaiah earlier that morning had been left to congeal on the plate.

The older man's mouth pinched into a flat line. "When I ask a question, I demand an answer." His voice was as loud and booming as it had always been, which made his sunken-in frame seem even smaller and insubstantial.

Dark circles ringed his eyes and sickly-pale skin sagged over his hollow cheeks. Even so, Jeremy had difficulty working up even a small bit of sympathy for the pitiful man lying in that bed.

Isaiah's poor health hadn't improved his disposition any.

There was no remorse for past actions, no wanting to make amends now that his time on earth was growing short. But then, for that to occur, he'd first have to admit that he'd actually done something wrong. And that was never going to happen.

Isaiah's eyes narrowed in a glower. "Did you stop somewhere along the way before coming home? It would be just like you to neglect your duties."

Jeremy clenched his teeth. It took everything in him not to hit back with angry words in return.

He had always been a hard worker, and he hadn't taken any time off for himself from the time he finished school at thirteen until he'd left the family farm at eighteen. All the while, he hadn't ever received a single word of acknowledgment or praise from his *daed*. Then, for the next five years, he'd worked from sunup to sundown on his leased farm in Illinois. He had never neglected his duties—not even when he would have much preferred to stay in Illinois instead of coming back here to Indiana—but he knew it was a useless endeavor to try to argue the point with Isaiah.

Jeremy unlocked his jaw to reply. "*Nee,* I came straight back here from the dry goods store."

He could admit to himself that he might have been delayed slightly by his encounter with Lovina. He'd been surprised by how much she still affected him, in spite of all the time that had passed. He'd found himself wanting to ask her at least a dozen questions, but he'd hesitated, and then the moment had been lost.

But the last person he would ever mention any of that to was the merciless man looking up at him right now with a scowl on his face.

Not for the first time, Jeremy wished he could have ignored the bishop's summons. Wished that there had been someone else available to take on this unpleasant responsibility. Being here again brought back too many unwanted memories.

If it had been Isaiah doing the asking—demanding—that Jeremy return to Baker's Corner and the family farm, maybe he could have shoved down any inconvenient twinges of his conscience and refused the command.

His four older brothers certainly hadn't had any problem turning their backs on the older man. Maybe Jeremy was being a bit unfair to them since they all had wives and children they couldn't just abandon for weeks on end—or however long Jeremy ended up being stuck here.

Except he wasn't entirely convinced that any of his brothers would have come to help Isaiah even if they didn't have a reasonable excuse to stay away. Not that Jeremy could find it in himself to blame them. He probably would have latched onto whatever excuse he could, if a legitimate one had been available to him.

He had prayed long and hard on the matter before finally

acknowledging that this was what *Gott* was guiding him to do. No matter that it went against Jeremy's inclination.

He might not want to be here, but that didn't change the fact that he was exactly where he needed to be. Walking to the bedside table, he picked up the dirty plate. "If I make you some soup, will you eat it?"

An obstinate look blanketed his *daed's* haggard features. "I want pot roast with potatoes and thick gravy. And an apple pie for dessert."

Jeremy knew that his father wouldn't be able to stomach such rich food and the pot roast and pie would go largely untouched, the same as the fried eggs and bacon Isaiah had demanded for breakfast. But Jeremy didn't voice any protest, well aware that if he tried to bring soup instead, Isaiah would simply refuse to eat it. Better that he pick at food that didn't sit well in his belly than to not eat anything at all.

Although at this rate, his *daed's* death would likely come sooner rather than later. Despite their differences—and Jeremy's longing to leave—he would never want a hand in hastening Isaiah's demise. The older man seemed determined to do it himself, however. And Jeremy didn't see that there was anything he could do to stop it.

He exited the room and carried the plate to the kitchen, where he dumped the contents into the trash bin. He quickly washed the dishes before setting to work preparing the roast. There wasn't time to make a pie given the list of chores he had waiting for him. He'd have to make another trip into town later to get the apple pie at the local bakery, as if Jeremy didn't have enough to do already, what with tending to the farm and the livestock while acting as nursemaid to his *daed*.

Trying to keep Isaiah happy had been an impossible task even before he was confined to his bed. Yet, Jeremy's stubborn pride refused to allow him to admit defeat.

He wondered if he might run into Lovina again when he visited her family's bakery later that day. He wasn't certain whether he hoped he would see her again or not. Although he couldn't deny his desire to spend more time in her company, it would be more prudent to keep his distance from her. His stay here was only a temporary one, and it would just cause him unnecessary pain if he allowed his feelings for Lovina to grow.

After he got the meat and vegetables into the oven, he headed outside to make a start on plowing the north field.

The day was hot and sweat soon rolled down his face, but it was a relief to be outside and away from the stifling atmosphere in the farmhouse. Even when his muscles started to ache, Jeremy didn't abandon the work.

And it had nothing to do with wanting to show Isaiah that he was a hard and diligent worker. Because Jeremy already knew that trying to prove anything to his father only led to disappointment.

Chapter Four

"What are you doing here?" The question popped out of Lovina's mouth before she could consider the wisdom of it.

Jeremy's sudden appearance at her family's bakery had left her so flustered that it was hard for her to think straight. She battled an almost overwhelming urge to order him out of the shop, but she couldn't turn away a potential customer just because he made her feel things she didn't want to feel. Taking in a deep breath, she struggled to regain a measure of calm, but was not entirely successful.

She hadn't expected to see him again so soon. She tried to convince herself that she didn't want to see him again only hours after their previous encounter, but the rapid beating of her heart belied that assurance and she couldn't delude herself, try though she might.

She was angry with herself that Jeremy could still affect her so strongly; in truth, that he had any sort of effect on her at all. If he felt similarly affected by her, he certainly gave no outward indication of it, which made it especially galling to face the fact that she couldn't seem to control her own response to him.

However, she resolved that she would not allow Jeremy to know the undeniable influence he still had on her.

Ignoring the prickling heat she could feel creeping into her cheeks, she squared her shoulders. "I mean, how can I help you?" she said in a bid to cover her earlier blunder.

"I'm in need of a pie," Jeremy responded, appearing completely unaware of the chaotic reactions he created inside her.

Lovina ran her damp palms down the apron covering her muted navy dress. "We have all kinds of pies here. Is there a particular flavor you had in mind?"

"Apple," he replied instantly. "Do you happen to have any available, by chance?"

She should know the answer to his question without needing to look, but suddenly every intelligent thought seemed to have flown from her head. Had they sold all the apple pies that had been baked earlier that day? She couldn't have said with any degree of certainty. Besides, she needed a moment away from Jeremy in order to attempt to regain her wits.

"Let me check over there." She waved vaguely toward the other side of the shop, then busied herself at the bakery case she'd indicated, taking far more time than was strictly required.

When she had delayed as long as she reasonably could without making it appear to be deliberate, she straightened up and moved back toward Jeremy with a pie tin in her hands. "You're in luck, we have one apple pie left. It was baked fresh this morning, and I'm sure you'll enjoy it."

For some reason that caused Jeremy's mouth to tighten into a grim line.

Although the odd reaction piqued her curiosity, she didn't want to prolong their interaction any longer than necessary by questioning him about it.

She boxed up the pie quickly, intent on hurrying him on his way.

A few minutes later he was gone—and contrarily, Lovina wished to have him back again. But she'd just have to get used to his absence, since he would be leaving town soon enough.

And this time, he'd be gone for good.

Lovina's steps were slow as she walked home later that afternoon. She knew that she should hurry. Her *mamm* would require help in preparing dinner. Lovina couldn't leave the older woman to struggle to do it on her own. Chopping vegetables and lifting heavy pots had become harder for her with the joints in her fingers crippled by arthritis. The damage made most tasks not only difficult, but painful as well.

If Lovina's *daed* was experiencing one of his lucid moments, which were becoming rarer and rarer with each day that passed, he would ask her to read the Bible aloud to him for a few minutes. Even when he didn't remember who she was, she still felt the need to share that time with him.

Then after dinner was done, there would be dishes to wash. Tomorrow, there was cleaning and dusting to do, laundry to wash and hang on the line, clothes in need of mending. It seemed that her list of chores was never-ending. Her *mamm* would help where she could, but the plain truth couldn't be ignored that the older woman wasn't able to do much any longer.

Lovina often felt exhausted and overwhelmed, but she couldn't allow herself to rest. There was simply too much to be done. Her love for her parents kept her pushing forward, despite aching muscles that felt as though they might give out. She had no choice but to continue putting one foot in front of the other. Over and over again.

She picked up her pace and quickly reached the house near the edge of town where she lived with her parents.

The paint on the wooden siding was peeling in spots and the

fence around the yard leaned at a precarious angle. Yet more things that required attention, but which Lovina never seemed to be able to find the time to tend to.

At least with all the tasks waiting for her, there would be little opportunity for unwanted thoughts of Jeremy to intrude.

Chapter Five

Lovina didn't see Jeremy for several days after that, and she tried to convince herself she was glad about that fact. The words seemed to ring hollow, however.

"Why did he have to come back?" she mumbled to herself, punching a lump of bread dough with more force than necessary.

"Why did who have to come back?" her brother asked, looking at her quizzically.

"No one."

John's eyebrows arched toward his hairline, but he didn't say anything further as he turned back to his own work and added dry ingredients to a large mixing bowl.

Lovina kneaded the dough, flipping it over and slapping it back down on the butcher-block countertop.

She wasn't done expressing her displeasure about Jeremy's recent arrival in town, but this time she made sure to keep her mumbling silent, so her brother wouldn't overhear.

Her life had been going along perfectly fine until he'd showed up. Sure, she'd been running herself ragged, but at least her heart hadn't been in any danger. That's not to say she thought it was in any danger now—maybe what she should have said was she hadn't had to deal with this agitation. Not that Jeremy bothered her, exactly. She refused to let him have that sort of power over her. But if he had no power over her, then why was she in such a state?

"Oh, why couldn't he have just stayed away?"

"Who?" John questioned.

Ach, she'd spoken that thought out loud. "No one," she repeated.

This was all Jeremy's fault.

He'd never gotten along well with his *daed*, so his sudden return to care for the older man seemed highly suspect. If he had left Baker's Corner to live in the *Englisch* world, maybe she could have understood Jeremy turning his back on Isaiah like he had when he'd left Baker's Corner. If Jeremy had turned *Englisch*, he would have been shunned by the older man—as had happened with two of Jeremy's brothers.

But three of the five Slagel brothers—Jeremy included—had continued in the Amish way of life, only they'd done so far away from here. Lovina simply could not comprehend how every single one of them had willfully abandoned their *daed*. Even when Isaiah first became sick, there had been no sign of his sons. Until now.

"Why did it have to be Jeremy?" If Samuel or Abraham Slagel had returned instead, she would be much happier right now.

Her life would have gone on as normal, at least.

A strand of hair came loose from the knot secured at her nape, and it fell in front of her eye. After brushing it aside with the back of her wrist, she gave the ball of bread dough a solid thump with the side of her fist.

"Lovina, who are you talking about?" Impatience tinged John's tone. He immediately held up a hand when she started to speak. "And don't say 'no one.'"

She snapped her mouth closed and glared at her older brother. "Fine, I won't say that."

He arched an eyebrow in silent inquiry, waiting for her to answer his question.

"Nobody."

He shook his head in exasperation, but at least he didn't question her again. "Well, your nobody is giving me a headache and the way you're pounding that dough, it's going to be inedible before too much longer."

Her lips pressed together in irritation. But she wasn't sure whether she was more frustrated with her brother or Jeremy. *Nee*, Jeremy was definitely the larger annoyance.

In town less than a week, and he was already causing problems for her. What were the odds she could avoid him for the rest of his stay here? Likely not good, given the size of Baker's Corner. But if she wanted to avoid him, why did she keep glancing out the front window of the bakery searching for him? Well, there could only be one reason for that. She needed to spot him first, so she could be certain to steer clear of him. That was the only logical explanation.

She nodded her head decisively, glad she had reasoned all of that out.

Jeremy exited the dry goods store and only narrowly avoided a painful collision with someone who was trying to enter. When he realized who it was, his heart reacted instantly. He greeted Lovina, and she responded in return, though her words sounded a bit stilted.

They spent the next several seconds locked in an awkward dance as they both stepped one way and then the other in an attempt to get out of each other's way.

Finally, he stopped and stood still, waiting for her to go around him. If there had been more room to maneuver, he suspected she would have given him a wide berth. Instead, she passed close enough to him for the hem of her dress to brush against the leg of his trousers. A moment later, she disappeared inside the store as the door swung shut behind her.

He shook his head at the peculiar exchange before continuing on his way.

Although he and Lovina had scarcely spoken, he'd felt the familiar tug toward her. He would've thought five years away should put an end to that, but clearly not.

He realized suddenly that this had been the third time he'd encountered her, and he had yet to ask her how she was doing. Nor had he asked about her parents, though he assumed she was still caring for them, the same as she had done before he'd left town when he turned eighteen.

He vowed to remedy that oversight on their next meeting.

Perhaps it would be wiser to keep his distance. But nothing would change his mind about heading back to Illinois when his obligations here were finished, so what harm could it do to spend a bit more time in Lovina's company? As long as he was careful to guard his heart against her, he'd have nothing to worry about. Well, nothing more than the pile of worries that were caused by the situation at his family's farm.

Chapter Six

A week later, Jeremy drove to Baker's Corner to buy more supplies at the dry goods store, but before returning to the farmhouse, he decided to take a walk through town.

He was greeted by several people, but not the one person he wanted to see. He tried not to appear too obvious as he passed the bakery and glanced inside. But he didn't see Lovina beyond the silver-colored lettering stenciled on the front window. Then she emerged from the back of the shop, heading toward the door. She turned her head to say something to her brother's wife, Mary, who was assisting customers.

When Lovina's gaze shifted forward once more, it landed on Jeremy standing outside. She stopped short and the smile slipped from her face as their gazes connected through the window glass. Then she seemed to collect herself and pulled open the door, stepping out onto the sidewalk.

Her greeting was stilted, but he didn't let that bother him—at least, not much. He fell into step beside her, ignoring the fact that she hadn't invited him to do so. He suspected he would've been waiting a long time before he received an invitation from her. In all likelihood, his return to Illinois would be happening sooner.

He knew it would be up to him to start the conversation. He didn't expect that she would say anything to him, unless it was to tell him to go away. Better to not give her the chance.

"We haven't had much opportunity to talk recently." He cringed at the inanity of the remark.

She leveled an incredulous look on him, but he was determined to forge ahead regardless. However, every question that came to mind sounded idiotic even in his own head.

This was proving to be more difficult than he expected, and he considered abandoning the effort. But as the alternative was returning to his family's farm, this seemed preferable. Even in her current mood, Lovina was a much more pleasant companion than his *daed*.

Lovina flicked a glance at him out of the corner of her eye. "I need to return home. My parents are expecting me."

He suspected that her words had been spoken with the intent

of brushing him off, but he seized the opening she'd given him. "How are your *mamm* and *daed?*"

She stopped suddenly in the middle of the sidewalk. She looked completely surprised at his question. "I... Are you really interested? Do you really care?"

He halted his steps as well. "Of course... I'm not—"

"But you left the first chance you had, so could you really be interested? You never were before."

He'd left because it was what he had to do to survive, but that didn't mean he had no regrets. "I'm here now."

"But why?"

"Is it truly so hard for you to believe that I might have some redeeming qualities?"

Although she didn't reply in words, he knew her answer.

He started to stalk off, but then turned back around to face her. "You're right that I might not want to be here. But I *am* here. Shouldn't that count for something? I had to put my own life on hold. I have a farm that I had to ask a neighbor to tend to in my absence, and I still have to pay the rent on the land. But I did it." He had worked up a good head of steam now. "I don't understand why you're so against me. You used to like me. What changed?"

"You did! When we were in school together, I thought you were my friend, but then it just...stopped." Her eyes closed for a brief second, then she shook her head. "Suddenly you were gone. And not because you left town. That didn't come until later. Afterward, you never visited, you never wrote."

He sighed and hung his head as several things became clear to him. Back then, he'd been too focused on his own struggles to realize what effect his actions had on anyone else. Even if he had known at the time, it might not have made any difference. He wasn't proud of that fact, but it was the truth.

He sighed and when he spoke again, his voice was softer. "I knew early on that I was going to leave, that I *had* to leave. I couldn't keep forming bonds I would have to sever." He'd fought against any ties that would bind him to Baker's Corner. The same thing held true now, he supposed. But in protecting himself, it seemed that he'd unintentionally hurt Lovina. "I never meant to hurt you. I'm sorry."

Her eyes misted over with tears. "Being sorry won't stop you from leaving again, though."

It wasn't a question, but he answered anyway. "*Nee.* But that doesn't mean we can't find a bit of common ground while I'm still here."

She swiped at her eyes. "What do we have in common?"

"More than you might think. You've been caring for your parents for years, and the only reason I'm back at the farm now is because my *daed* has need of me." Though it wasn't Jeremy specifically who was needed.

Frankly, Isaiah would probably prefer someone else. But neither of them had any choice in the matter.

In the beginning, a few of Isaiah's neighbors had tried to help out, but his father had managed to chase them all away with his insults and demands. Jeremy didn't have the money to hire anyone. If he did, he might have been able to fulfill his duty from afar while remaining in Illinois. But even paying somebody a wage was no guarantee that they would stay and suffer through Isaiah's verbal abuses.

Lovina's parents were much kinder, he knew. "Have you considered hiring someone to help you?"

"*Nee.*"

"Why not, Lovina? Between working at the bakery and taking care of your parents, you must be exhausted. Do you have any time for yourself?"

"I-I don't need time for myself. I like helping my parents. They're not a burden to me."

He took a step closer, and his gaze on her was soft. "But surely, you must get tired and want to take a short rest now and then." Jeremy himself certainly felt that way while trying to do more work than any one person could handle.

Even though Lovina's parents were nowhere near as difficult as his father, caring for ill family members took a lot out of a person. And a person could only do so much, as Jeremy had reason to know firsthand, what with all the responsibilities that had been heaped on his shoulders since he'd returned to his family's farm.

"I'm fine. I don't need any help," Lovina told him. "I-I'm doing just fine on my own."

A sudden wave of sadness filled Jeremy upon hearing her words.

Chapter Seven

Lovina's exhaustion made her temper flare at Jeremy's implied criticism. Was he actually doubting that she was caring for her parents properly? Of course, there were times when she was tired and worn out, but that affected her, not them. She never allowed her feelings to interfere with caring for her *mamm* and her *daed*.

She didn't view it as a sacrifice because she loved them. It didn't matter to her that she had little time to herself and wasn't able to participate in the normal activities that other young women her age took for granted. That wasn't important.

She knew Jeremy hadn't hired any help, and he had an entire farm full of chores he was tackling on his own. So why should he suggest *she* get help?

"There's nothing wrong with hiring help," Jeremy mentioned again, which only riled her up more.

"Of course, you would say that. And that's because you don't want to be here," she turned his words back on him. "You'd rather be anywhere else. But I love my parents. Taking care of them is not a sacrifice. It didn't take my *daed* almost dying before I came home because I never left in the first place. I would *never* leave. You—" She cut herself off abruptly, horrified at her words. She'd said too much—she was out of control.

Jeremy's expression blanked, and his eyes were an icy blue. "You're not wrong. About any of it."

Lovina bit down hard on her lower lip, regretting her hurtful words. She'd implied he was not a good son. And she'd as good as said that he didn't love his *daed*.

He turned on his heels and started to walk away from her.

"Jeremy, wait. I didn't mean that."

If he heard her, he pretended otherwise.

"Jeremy!" she called after him.

He didn't break stride or look back. Then he was gone, before she could gather her wits enough to run after him and stammer out an apology.

She turned in the opposite direction.

Suddenly, she noticed a gaping hole in her logic. If Jeremy didn't want to be in Baker's Corner, then why hadn't he hired a farm hand or someone to tend to his father? If he had the money, surely he wouldn't be doing all the work himself. And since he *was* doing all the work himself, it must be because he had no alternative.

Except that wasn't actually true. No one had physically forced him back to Indiana. He could have stayed in Illinois and turned a blind eye to his *daed's* illness. But he'd made a different choice.

Which meant... Jeremy's actions were proof that he wasn't the type of man who turned his back on his family when his help was needed.

Groaning at her insensitivity and just plain rudeness, she slowly started trudging home.

That night Lovina fell into bed, exhausted after another long day working nonstop—except for that disastrous walk with Jeremy. Other than that, she'd scarcely had a spare moment to even pause in order to catch her breath. Yet, she was unable to fall asleep as her conversation with Jeremy continued to circle in her head.

Now that a haze of heightened emotions no longer clouded her judgment, she was able to ponder his words. And she could acknowledge that his suggestion of hiring help was worth considering.

He was right that it had all started to feel like a bit too much for her, though she hadn't wanted to admit it. And when she thought about the fact that things would only become more difficult as time passed and her parents got older... No one expected her to do everything. No one except herself.

Her brothers—and their wives—had encouraged her to speak up if there was ever anything she needed from them. Knowing they were busy with the bakery and their young children, she hadn't wanted to burden them.

It wasn't shameful to admit that she needed help, however. That she couldn't handle it all on her own. Such an admission didn't make her a bad daughter or a bad person.

She didn't want to put more work on her brothers or sisters-in-law, but the family could afford to hire someone to help out at the house for a few hours each day. Another person who could take on a portion of the cooking and the cleaning, or just to give Lovina a short break.

Having reached that conclusion, she shared her plans with her *mamm* the next morning during breakfast, after she'd already delivered a tray to her *daed*. He hadn't yet risen from bed, and he may or may not have been cognizant enough to take part in the conversation, in any case.

The older woman wrung her hands, dismay flitting across her

face. "Oh, I don't know if that's a good idea, Lovina. It might be too upsetting for your *daed*."

"But we're struggling," Lovina pointed out as gently as she could, not wanting to draw too much attention to her *mamm's* health issues.

"I've done my best to help you." Her mother's arthritic-twisted fingers plucked a loose thread in the tablecloth, standing out starkly against the dark blue, checked fabric.

"I know that, *Mamm*." Lovina reached out to lay her hand over the older woman's. "I do. But surely, you must realize that we can't continue on this way?"

Her mother lowered her gaze to her hands and nodded just once.

Taking that as agreement to hiring some help, Lovina began looking for a suitable person that very day.

When she mentioned her intention to her brother's wife while at the bakery, she suggested her teenage niece, Ruth, who just so happened to live only a few houses away from Lovina and her parents. The close proximity would certainly prove convenient, and Lovina promised to consider the girl if she indicated she was interested in the job.

Ruth was a sweet, quiet girl of about fifteen, and she accepted the job as soon as Lovina finished giving her all the details. They arranged for her to start the next day. When they parted, Lovina was left with a feeling of optimism. She prayed that things would work out with Ruth.

It didn't take long to come to appreciate Ruth's helpful presence. Lovina felt as though a weight had been lifted from her shoulders. A weight she hadn't wanted to even admit was there in the first place.

With Ruth lending some welcome assistance, it afforded Lovina the opportunity to just sit and talk with her parents, instead of rushing off to see to an endless list of chores.

Those shared moments were especially precious with her *daed* because she knew his memories were fading as his condition continued to worsen. So, she cherished the time they had together now—while his good days still outnumbered the bad ones.

She owed Jeremy a debt of gratitude for forcing her to face the truth. Although she hadn't taken kindly to his candor at the time, it had been sorely needed.

A few days later, Lovina spotted Jeremy in town during his weekly trip to the dry goods store and she hurried over to talk to him.

"I wanted to say *denki*, Jeremy."

His eyebrows pulled together. "For what? I haven't done anything worthy of thanks."

"That's not true. You helped me to see that another set of

hands would be of benefit to my parents as much as to me." She'd since learned that her *mamm* had been attempting to take on too much since she could see Lovina's exhaustion and felt compelled to try to lighten the load for her daughter. "I knew that *Mamm's* arthritis gave her more trouble at the end of the day, but I hadn't realized she was pushing herself more than she should because of me."

Lovina felt extremely guilty for that, and it wasn't the only thing that had caused her guilt recently. "I owe you an apology for the way I behaved the other day."

"There's no need to apologize."

Although, she wanted to protest, she didn't push him on the subject. She didn't wish to start another ridiculous argument that would be entirely her fault.

Instead, she focused on the good Ruth had done for her parents. "After I hired Ruth to help me, I noticed an improvement in the situation in just a handful of days."

He smiled, sharing in her lighter mood. "I'm pleased to hear it."

Unfortunately, Ruth wasn't able to bring a similar improvement to Lovina's *daed's* deteriorating mental state.

Lovina's brief moment of happiness faded at the unwelcome thought. "I feared having a stranger in the house might upset *Daed*. But when his memory is clear, he knows Ruth and seems to enjoy her company. On the days when he forgets things...he sometimes mistakes *me* for a stranger then." She tried to laugh off that last part, but it hurt that there were times when her *daed* didn't know her.

And she knew he wasn't going to get any better. He had good days and bad days. But there would likely come a time when he couldn't remember his loved ones at all.

She pushed the grim thoughts from her mind, determined not to dwell on them any longer.

At that moment, Jeremy's friendly support meant much to her. He had helped to lighten the weight of responsibility on her shoulders, despite dealing with his own troubles. She wanted to offer him something in return, even if it was just a small thing.

"Would you like to join my family for supper this evening," she invited.

He looked surprised at her invitation before he shook his head. "*Nee.* I need to be getting back to the farm. I can't leave my *daed* for too long alone."

Lovina tried not to let her disappointment show. Though she had hoped for a different response, she understood his refusal. He had responsibilities of his own. Unlike her, he didn't have his brothers nearby to step in if he faltered.

"I won't delay you any longer, then."

Only after he was gone—when it was too late to try to offer

him another apology—did it occur to her that his refusal served as a much-needed reminder that he intended to leave Baker's Corner soon—a fact she had allowed herself to forget for a short while. She reminded herself that she couldn't let Jeremy any further into her heart.

She just hoped that it wasn't already too late to avoid heartbreak this time.

The drive back to the farmhouse gave Jeremy more time to think than was to his liking. Trapped alone in his head with nothing to distract him, his conscience started to prod him.

He thought back to his conversation with Lovina a few days before. Although what he'd given as his reason for cutting his connection to her those five years ago was true enough, it wasn't the whole truth. His departure had to do with more than just a pressing need to escape Baker's Corner. Self-preservation had compelled him to cut their ties—in order to keep Lovina from getting too close. To keep her from working her way completely into his heart. It hadn't been wise to spend any more time with her—or he might not have been able to leave.

And he *had* to leave.

He wondered if she had seen through his excuse. Not that he believed she might've guessed his underlying motive. He hadn't even been aware of it himself at the time. But she knew that there was no love lost between him and his *daed*. But she didn't know the truth of it. She didn't know that his father was a man who would berate and belittle him at every possible moment.

Something he'd continued to do from the moment Jeremy arrived back at the farmhouse. He never planned to remain in Baker's Corner for long. And that hadn't changed in the weeks he'd been here.

But leaving Lovina might not be as easy as it was the first time—and back then, it had been much harder than he'd ever imagined. If he didn't put some distant between them now, it might prove impossible, and he couldn't let that happen.

Because he wasn't willing to stay here forever. Not even for her.

Chapter Eight

Jeremy knew his *daed* was failing. In truth, he was worsening much more quickly than Jeremy would have imagined when he'd first arrived. But the evidence was clear. His father was hardly eating anything, and his raking voice had faded in strength. Jeremy wondered how many more weeks or even days he would last.

He needed to find a way to forgive the older man before it was too late. Not for Isaiah's sake, but for his own. If Jeremy ever hoped to find peace, this was something he had to do. Otherwise, he would be forced to live with regret for the rest of his life. And he'd already spent enough years mired in bitterness and anger.

That night he sat down at his *daed's* bedside. He didn't allow his father's insults and tirades to drive him away.

"I forgive you," Jeremy said, though it seemed to stick in his throat.

He wasn't sure in that moment whether it was the truth or a lie, but he'd needed to say the words so he would have no regrets that they'd been left unspoken.

"Have you said all you needed to say?" Isaiah demanded weakly with a sneer on his emaciated face.

"*Jah.*" Jeremy stiffened. His words had obviously been a waste of his breath.

"Well, then let me tell *you* something. I don't need your forgiveness. Nothing I did was wrong. You hear me! Who are you to judge me? I broke my back to provide for you. Food, clothing, a roof over your head. And did I ever hear a word of thanks from you or your brothers? Not a one. Ungrateful, the whole lot of you!" He condemned all five of his sons with rasping breath. "Get out of my sight. I don't need you hovering above me like a vulture waiting to pick over my carcass as soon as I die."

Jeremy was more than happy to leave. Pushing to his feet, he exited the room without sparing the older man another glance.

Except leaving the room wasn't far enough away from Isaiah to suit Jeremy, so he headed out to the barn. The animals didn't really need tending, but Jeremy couldn't bear to stay in the farmhouse for another moment.

He started to muck out the stalls but slammed the handle of the pitchfork back down a moment later, fearing he'd do himself damage if he continued stabbing the sharp tines into the ground near his feet while he was in a temper.

Isaiah's diatribe kept repeating in Jeremy's head, ratcheting up his anger even more, though he tried to suppress it and not let the harsh words eat at him.

Of course, his father wouldn't make it easy for him. Of course, he would refuse to take any responsibility for the large part he'd played in the vast rift between them. Jeremy would have been a fool to ever expect otherwise.

He paced up and down the space between the stalls, then walked out the back door of the barn and looked out over the fields of crops and pastures filled with knee-high grass. The view hadn't changed much since he'd been a kid.

"And it seems like nothing else has changed here either."

Jeremy was a grown man, and yet his *daed* could still get under his skin and make him feel like he was that miserable young boy again, forced to listen to Isaiah berate him because his chores hadn't been done "right." Not that the chores hadn't been finished, but they weren't done according to Isaiah's dictates. Because in Isaiah Slagel's mind, there were only two ways of doing things—his way and the wrong way.

Jeremy closed his eyes and breathed deeply, searching within himself for the patience and strength he needed.

Finally, he forced himself back to the farmhouse to check on Isaiah, but something was wrong. A strange twisted look was imprinted on the old man's face. His heart lurching, Jeremy moved closer. His father's face was frozen in place—the only slackness being the way his jaw fell against his neck. Without touching him to check, Jeremy knew.

He was gone. Dead. Slumping down onto the chair next to his *daed's* lifeless body, Jeremy put his head in his hands.

He wanted to feel sorrow, but he just felt numb. Though the guilt came before long. Strangely, the relief he'd expected to feel in this moment didn't come. He had nearly succeeded in convincing himself that he hated the older man for the way he'd treated Jeremy all his life. The truth wasn't as simple as that, however.

No matter Isaiah's faults, he hadn't managed to completely kill Jeremy's love for him. Jeremy groaned and let his tears fall.

Lovina was working at the bakery when she heard the news of Isaiah Slagel's passing. She wanted to offer Jeremy comfort, but he'd continued to stay out on the farm and hadn't come into town in several days. She considered asking one of her brothers to drive her out to the farmhouse to see him, but it didn't seem right to intrude on his grief without an invitation.

She found herself considering what to do, as she kneaded

bread dough. "I want to support him, but how can I do that from a distance?"

"Who?" John's wife, Mary questioned, laying strips of pie dough in a lattice pattern over a pie tin of apple filling.

"Nobody."

"Is this the same nobody you were talking about a few weeks ago?" Mary asked.

Lovina twisted around to look at her sister-in-law. "How do you know about that?"

"John told me. Can you believe he couldn't figure out it was Jeremy Slagel?" she said with a laugh.

Lovina felt her cheeks heating. "So, John knows, too, now?"

Mary looked at her with concern. "Was it supposed to be a secret?"

"Well, *nee*, but..." She shook her head. "Never mind." She resumed kneading the dough. "So, can I assume you and John will stop doing owl impersonations from now on?"

Mary's nose wrinkled in confusion. "What?"

"Who? Who? Sounds like, hoo, hoo," she explained.

The other woman laughed, and Lovina found herself smiling in response.

Mary dusted flour off her hands. "John's going to love hearing this story."

Lovina's hands rested on the butcher-block counter. "Why do you have to tell him everything?"

Mary only laughed again, as she transferred the pie into the oven and left the bakery.

Lovina's thoughts immediately circled back to Jeremy.

It had been a few days since his *daed's* passing and Jeremy was still in town. Of course, the funeral wasn't until tomorrow, and Jeremy wouldn't leave before that. Would he depart the next day? She couldn't help but hope that he might decide to stay longer.

With all her heart, she hoped he might decide he never wanted to return to Illinois—no matter how unlikely that hope seemed.

Chapter Nine

Unable to look at the simple pine coffin any longer, as it was lowered into the ground, Jeremy focused his gaze on the horizon. There was not a cloud in the sky, the blue color so bright that it almost hurt his eyes.

It was a beautiful day, at odds with the somber occasion. But then, though the memories shamed him now, there had been many times as a young boy that Jeremy had imagined he'd be celebrating when this day finally came. The boy he'd been had not expected to spend a single moment mourning his *daed's* passing.

The truth was something far different, however.

The sun shone brightly overhead, causing Jeremy to sweat beneath his heavy black coat. Or perhaps that had more to do with his uncomfortable feelings than the warm temperature.

A slight breeze blew across the hillside, but it offered little relief.

The smell of fresh-cut hay from a nearby field lingered in the air, and birds tweeted and chirped in the trees along the fence line.

Jeremy glanced over at his two older brothers, Samuel and Abraham, standing next to him. Neither displayed any emotion, both wearing blank expressions. He wondered if they truly didn't feel anything at all—or if they were simply better at hiding it than he was.

Jeremy didn't want to feel anything, but there was no denying the turmoil of conflicting emotions inside him. Mostly it was anger and bitterness; however, he could not ignore the small sliver of grief mixed in with the harsher feelings he'd always felt toward his *daed*.

Although Jeremy had told Isaiah that he forgave him, now he had to face the shameful fact that it wasn't actually the truth. Maybe he would never be able to forgive him—which surely made Jeremy no better than the older man.

As soon as the service was over, his two older brothers walked away from the gravesite without a backward glance. They didn't even bother to return to the farmhouse for the funeral dinner.

At least, they had come—which was more than his other two brothers had done. But then, they hadn't just left the family farm when they were old enough. They'd left the Amish way of life behind, too, severing all connections to their past save one—Jeremy and their other brothers. However, that brotherly bond had not stretched to coming back here, not even now that Isaiah was gone.

Jeremy would have liked the support of all his brothers to help him get through this day, but two were better than none. Even if all Samuel and Abraham offered him was their silent presence at his side; he was just glad that he wasn't completely alone.

"Are you going to come back to the farmhouse?" Jeremy had asked his brothers as they walked toward the horse-drawn buggies parked along the side of the road.

"*Nee*, I need to set out now," Abraham replied. "It's a long drive, and I want to make it back home tonight."

"I'd best be getting on home, too," Samuel seconded.

Jeremy's steps faltered. "So, you're leaving already? Before the meal?"

Samuel turned back to look at him. "That's no reason for us to stay."

Their words shouldn't have come as a shock to Jeremy. But still, they hurt.

"There's no reason for you to stay either, Jeremy," Abraham

added more gently. "You can finally leave here and return to Illinois."

"But what about our family farm?" Jeremy didn't know what he wanted to do about it, but it wasn't his decision alone to make.

Although Isaiah had never bothered with a will or written instructions, now that he was gone, the farm belonged to all five of his sons collectively. No matter that it was a painful legacy...

Jeremy looked at both of his brothers in turn. "We can't just abandon it."

Abraham's mouth turned down at the corners. "Why not? I know I don't want anything to do with that farm."

"Neither do I." Samuel crossed his arms over his chest, his expression hard.

Jeremy knew there was no sense in even bringing their other two brothers into this discussion. Their absence was all the answer he needed as to their feelings on the subject. They had no love for the place where they'd grown up.

"And I don't think you truly want it either, Jeremy. Or am I wrong?" Abraham asked.

"I—" After all the hours of backbreaking work he'd put in over the past several weeks, was he really willing to let it go?

But it wasn't as though he *wanted* to keep the farm now that there was nothing to hold him here any longer. Did he? Surely, he wasn't actually contemplating the possibility of staying.

No, he wasn't—except…Lovina was here.

Along with a host of painful memories and unwanted reminders of the past, he told himself grimly.

Samuel kicked at a clump of grass with his foot. "The farm can fall into ruin for all I care. In fact, if you want my opinion, I suggest we let it do just that."

Jeremy shook his head, though it wasn't necessarily in disagreement to his brother's statement. However, until he could figure out exactly what his feelings were, it would be no use trying to argue the matter.

Chapter Ten

The next day, Jeremy felt restless. Uncertain. He couldn't quite bring himself to hang around the farmhouse alone just yet. So, he made his way into Baker's Corner and wandered around aimlessly for a time until he found himself standing on the sidewalk in front of the bakery owned by Lovina's family.

Pushing open the door, he stepped inside and glanced around. It only took him an instant to ascertain that Lovina was nowhere in sight. Instead, her oldest brother, John stood behind the glass display cases filled with assorted baked goods.

"If you're looking for Lovina, she left just a few minutes ago. You can probably catch up with her if you hurry," the other man said by way of a greeting.

The comment pulled Jeremy up short. Had his recent preoccupation with Lovina been so obvious that even her family had taken note of it? Or had Lovina mentioned him to her family? Did John's words mean that Lovina felt something for him, too?

As much as that possibility caused a jolt of joy to pierce his heart, he cautioned himself against reading too much into a single offhand remark. A moment later, the thought was crowded out by another one.

Had he been subconsciously seeking out Lovina now?

He suddenly wondered how much of his hesitation to make a decision about the farm might have to do with Lovina and not wanting to leave her. Surely, he wasn't secretly hoping she would give him a reason to stay.

He wanted to put the past behind him. But that would mean leaving Baker's Corner. Leaving Lovina. There was no denying that the thought of it caused a sharp pang in his chest.

The thought of living with constant reminders of his past caused him just as much pain, however. Perhaps it would be better not to see Lovina until he could work out in his own mind what he truly wanted.

His good intentions turned to ash, however, when he stepped outside and spotted Lovina exiting the dry goods store. She hadn't caught sight of him yet, and he should turn in the other direction and disappear before she had a chance to see him standing here. He couldn't seem to make his feet move, however. Couldn't quite convince himself to keep his distance. His head knew, of course, that he should walk away right now —for both of their sakes—but his heart seemed intent on ignoring the commands from his brain.

And then it was too late as he watched her eyes brighten when she noticed him standing motionless on the sidewalk in front of her family's bakery.

She seemed happy to see him—which brought Jeremy equal parts joy and regret. It pleased him to see proof that she felt a similar pull toward him as he felt toward her, as though they were magnets being drawn together. But at the same time, his conscience prodded him to flee before he disappointed her somehow and stole the smile from her face.

Before she discovered he was not the good man she hopefully believed him to be.

She was already walking toward him, however, and he couldn't pretend he hadn't seen her or hurt her by not acknowledging her. Although sometimes pain was unavoidable, he had never held with the notion of being knowingly cruel.

Returning Lovina's bright greeting, he stuffed his thumbs under his suspenders. Her expression sobered and he fought not to fidget when she offered her condolences, compassion softening her gaze.

"I'm sorry to hear of your *daed's* passing. If there's anything you need, I hope you'll let me know."

"There's nothing," he denied. At least, nothing that anyone else could give him. "The women of the district brought over a lot of food."

"I was there," she said softly. "Even though you didn't see me."

"You were?" he questioned. He wasn't sure how in the world he'd missed her presence there. He supposed he was too preoccupied with his brothers.

"I didn't stay afterward," she said. "You looked busy enough."

"Thank you for coming."

"You're welcome."

He gazed at her face, at her peaceful look, and he yearned for the same.

Acceptance of his past, forgiveness for his *daed*, an easing of the guilt Jeremy felt for the estrangement between them that was there even on the day Isaiah died—all the things he knew were required for him to know peace but which continued to elude him, seeming just out of his reach. They could only be found within himself and with *Gott's* help. And he might not even be able to find them there, if he was being honest.

"What are you going to do about your family farm?" Lovina asked the question he'd been asking himself only a short while before.

He still didn't have the answer. "I don't know. None of my brothers have any interest in it."

Samuel and Abraham had made that plain to him. They didn't care what happened to the farm. Jeremy didn't want to care either, but he couldn't seem to cut off his emotions, though that would have certainly made this whole situation much easier for him.

He should make a start on clearing out his *daed's* belongings, at least. If none of them wanted anything to do with the farm, then the obvious solution would be to sell it and split the proceeds. But Jeremy couldn't quite make himself take that step just yet.

He knew he would have to decide what to do about the farm at some point, however.

Without warning, he experienced a sudden flash of temper that his brothers had left him to deal with this by himself, the same way they'd left him to tend to the farm and their *daed* single-handedly during Isaiah's last days. Although, to be fair, in the case of their inheritance, it wasn't as though his brothers actually expected Jeremy to do anything about it.

Lovina was studying him, and he wondered whether she could sense the turmoil in his mind. But he couldn't stop his thoughts, couldn't stop the flood of confusion assailing him.

Maybe it would be better for everyone if he just abandoned the place, as Samuel had suggested. But Jeremy found that he couldn't simply ignore everything in his past, as though none of it had ever happened. Even when he tried to put it from his mind, it was always there. There was no escaping that fact. He had to face it. He might be able to pretend like none of it mattered to him—and maybe others would even believe him—but there was no fooling himself.

"Do you have any interest in the farm?" Lovina asked after waiting patiently, an odd note in her voice.

But his head was too full of grim thoughts to try to figure out the cause of her tone.

Rather than attempting to explain his tangled feelings, however, he focused on the practical instead. "I need to return to my leased farm in Illinois. My neighbor has been keeping an eye on it for me, but it's time for that arrangement to end now that I no longer need to stay here."

Her green eyes seemed to dim a bit. Or maybe that was just Jeremy's imagination.

A few strands of hair had come loose from the knot at the back of Lovina's head, and she tucked them behind her ear. "I guess you'll be leaving soon then."

"*Jah.*" That had always been the plan—yet suddenly, he didn't want to go.

But although he was coming to hate the thought of leaving Lovina, he feared that there were too many raw memories of this place for him to ever be able to make a life for himself here free from the bitterness of his past.

Lovina bit down on her lip and then spoke again. "When will you set out on your journey back to Illinois?"

He shook his head, not knowing the answer to that question either.

Would she be sorry to see him go? He knew he would miss her. Did he want her to miss him, too? It caused a sharp stab of pain to think that she might be hurt by his departure. Wasn't he done hurting her?

But he had never intended to linger in Baker's Corner once his duty was done. Yet leaving here again would not be quite as easy as he'd always expected it to be.

Stay or go? What was the best way forward? Which one could he live with afterward? Leaving might seem the easier choice, but was it really? Or would he wake up each day for the rest of his life regretting that decision?

Again, Lovina waited patiently while his thoughts swirled.

"I, uh, I don't know for certain," he said, knowing his answer was lame and made him sound weak.

"Oh," she said so softly he barely heard her.

"I'll tell you something, though," he said quickly. "This time, I won't leave without saying *gut*-bye. Not this time."

Her eyes filled with tears, and she nodded. "I-I should get going," she said. "Bye for now, Jeremy."

"Bye for now," he answered, feeling something in him crack. He turned away quickly, fearing he would weep right there on the street in plain sight of anyone coming along.

Chapter Eleven

Returning to the farmhouse a short time later, it felt as though the memories were pressing down on Jeremy, overwhelming him and making it difficult to breathe. There were too many oppressive memories locked within these walls to ever consider living here again—which meant his decision had been made.

He couldn't even stomach the task of going through Isaiah's belongings at the moment. Maybe in a few months. But not now.

Tomorrow morning, Jeremy would pack up his own things and head back to Illinois—*before* his affection for Lovina grew any greater. Before whatever affection she felt for him had a chance to turn into something more. He didn't want to hurt her any more than he already had.

It was time for him to return to the leased farm he now called home. A farm far away from Baker's Corner.

It should have felt like a relief. Yet, now that the moment was upon him, it didn't bring him any joy.

After a restless night spent tossing and turning in bed, Jeremy wrote a letter to Lovina, telling her good-bye. He'd promised to let her know, and he was going to make sure that he did. Part of him recoiled at telling her in a letter, but he didn't waver. If he told her in person, he might weaken. He did not want to weaken. He mailed the letter and then loaded his meager possessions into his hired driver's van. Without any fuss, they drove away from the farmhouse. As the van passed through Baker's Corner, a few people waved to Jeremy. He nodded to them in return, but of course, he didn't stop to talk to anyone.

He found himself hoping to catch one last glimpse of Lovina before he headed out of town, but he didn't see her. Which of course, was better.

Gripping the armrest of the van, he stared out the side window. They continued down the highway until the van crested a hill. As the town disappeared from sight, he didn't know when he would be back this way again. Maybe he'd never come back.

Coming to Baker's Corner this time had been hard enough.

He wanted to believe that he was strong enough to come back

and sort through his father's belongings once he had gained a bit of distance from the turmoil of the past several weeks. But he was honest enough with himself to acknowledge that there was a fair chance he might not be able to force himself to return here ever again, no matter the unresolved issues with the farm.

Gott alone knew. Jeremy didn't feel any certainty on that point at the moment.

"I saw Jeremy Slagel leaving town," Ruth commented as she and Lovina worked together to prepare breakfast for Lovina's parents.

"What?" Lovina gasped, turning to look at the younger girl. "When?"

"While I was walking here a short time ago." Ruth continued cracking open eggs against the side of a ceramic bowl, seeming unaware of the turmoil she'd caused with only a few words. "I'm pretty sure it was him, anyway. He was in a white van."

Lovina felt as though her heart has just been cracked open like one of those eggs.

She wanted to run outside and try to catch him, but she knew it was much too late for that. He was gone.

He promised me, she thought. *He promised he'd say gut-bye.*

She turned her face away, so that Ruth couldn't see her expression. Tears welled up in her eyes, and she blinked rapidly to try to stem them.

She couldn't believe that he was truly gone, that he'd left Baker's Corner without saying a single word to her, not after his promise. Why hadn't he just told her yesterday that he was planning to leave this morning?

But why should she be surprised? She'd known it was only a matter of time before it happened. Just as she'd known all along that it had been unwise to ever think otherwise. It didn't matter that her heart yearned for impossible things.

But she'd expected he would fulfill his promise, at least.

It became clear to her at that moment, that he didn't feel any strong emotions for her, nothing like the growing affection she felt for him. He had not been coming to care deeply for her, as she'd foolishly allowed herself to hope.

Only right then did she acknowledge she had actually started to believe he might decide to stay. But she had built those dreams on a foundation of nothing. He had never indicated a change of heart. At least, not overtly. She'd imagined that she had seen signs. But obviously she'd read much more into Jeremy's actions than had been warranted.

Well, she wouldn't make that mistake again. Never, ever, ever again.

She couldn't deny the sudden sharp pain she felt at the thought of never seeing him again, even though it meant she wouldn't have to risk another heartache.

Later, when she received his letter, she hardly wanted to open it. She'd steeled her heart against him and didn't relish opening herself to more pain. But in the end, she opened it and read his cursory good-bye.

It didn't make her feel better at all. In truth, it made her feel worse.

Chapter Twelve

Jeremy had not been back in Illinois a full day before he began to second-guess his decision to leave Baker's Corner. Yesterday, it had seemed like the best course to take, the *only* course, but... had he acted too hastily? Walked away because it was easier, rather than because it was the right thing to do?

And piled on top of his doubts was his growing regret at leaving Lovina. He missed her even more than he had imagined. But what could he do about it?

There was nothing to stop him from going back to Indiana—except his desire to avoid reopening the wounds of the past. Besides, he had neglected his leased farm for long enough. He'd only just returned. He couldn't turn right back around again and leave so soon. Or was that merely an excuse?

Nee, he had responsibilities here.

But you have responsibilities at the family farm in Baker's Corner, too.

He tried to push the thought from his head. There was no ignoring his duty, however, just as there had been no ignoring the summons from the bishop that had taken him back to Baker's Corner in the first place.

He didn't know what to do. He was being pulled in two different directions. And he had no idea as to which one would win out in the end.

A few days later, he was no closer to making sense of his conflicted feelings. He found himself writing a letter to Lovina, although he didn't put any of his jumbled thoughts down on the paper.

Still, his heart felt a bit lighter at this renewed connection to her, tenuous though it was.

"What's that, dear?" Lovina's *mamm* asked, staring at the sealed envelope that Lovina held in her hand.

"A letter from Jeremy Slagel," she replied.

The surprise on the older woman's face matched the emotion Lovina was feeling. Why had Jeremy written to her? She turned over the envelope, as though that would provide some heretofore-unnoticed clue about what might be contained inside. But there was only one way to find out.

Lovina excused herself and went to her room, shutting the door behind her before she torn open the envelope. She pulled the sheet of paper out and scanned the contents, then read his words slowly and carefully.

Dear Lovina,

I hope this finds you well. By now, you will have learned from my previous letter that I returned to my farm in Illinois. I felt obligated to return, as I have responsibilities here.

The neighbor who took over for me while I was gone did a fine job. The crops are coming along well, which is gratifying to see.

Might I say once again how happy I am that you have help now. It must continue to be a real blessing to you. Well, I will close for now. I trust all is well with your family.

Your friend,

Jeremy

Lovina sighed. Nothing personal at all, and it seemed that he was settling back into his life there. So then, why had he felt an urge to stay in contact with her now, when he hadn't written her a single letter during the five years he'd been gone before?

She had tried to continue with her normal routine and had

put thoughts of him from her mind since he'd left, but she'd failed miserably. She found herself missing him, though she didn't want to. And she feared that this feeling of missing him would never change. This letter certainly did nothing to help her forget him. Just the opposite, in fact.

That didn't stop her from writing back to him, however. And she responded to every other letter he sent to her over the course of the next few weeks.

But she refused to allow her heart to start hoping again.

She'd simply have to come to terms with the fact that he wouldn't be coming back. Ever. Because there was no reason for him to do so. Certainly not for her. If he aimed to sell his family farm—as she suspected was his intention—that could be dealt with from a distance.

The fact that she was still here wouldn't make any difference to him at all.

Jeremy was pleased to receive a reply from Lovina, and they exchanged half a dozen letters after that. Each one caused a mix of emotions, however. Even a simple account of her day could bring a smile to his face, but it also made him miss her more.

As the days passed, his thoughts turned to her with ever increasing frequency. So much so that he began to contemplate asking her to consider a move to Illinois. His leased farm was doing well, and he would be able to comfortably support a wife and family. Several members of the local Amish church had made comments on that subject recently. However, none of the women here had inspired him to give serious consideration to taking a wife, but with Lovina, the prospect suddenly held a much greater appeal.

Almost as soon as the idea entered his head, however, he was forced to discard it. Lovina would never agree to leave Baker's Corner. Or more accurately, she'd never agree to abandon her duty to her parents. And rightly so.

She didn't have the contentious relationship with her parents Jeremy had had with Isaiah. He remembered how at first, Lovina had balked at having help in for just a few hours a day. And though she had given in on that point eventually, she'd made it plain that she would never willingly leave her *mamm* and *daed* and move to another state. Besides, Jeremy would never want to come between Lovina and her family—and that had nothing to do with the fact that if it came down to a choice between him or them, he knew he would always come out on the losing end.

Suggesting her parents make the move with her was simply not an option. Even though her *daed's* memories were hazy and confused, it would be cruel to take him from his familiar surroundings.

As much as Jeremy wanted Lovina to share his life here, there was no way he could ask that of her. No way she'd ever consider it, even assuming she felt strong enough emotion for him to be interested in uprooting her own life in the first place.

Which meant he was still left with a bit of a dilemma— especially when he realized that he wanted to be back with her again more than he wanted to continue avoiding reminders of the life he'd once known in Indiana.

He needed to stop running from his past. He hadn't truly been able to escape it even when he'd moved hundreds of miles away. Maybe it was time to return to Baker's Corner and face the ghosts that haunted him. Maybe it was time to lay them to rest at last.

Maybe it was time to understand the true meaning of forgiveness.

Would Lovina want to be a part of whatever life Jeremy made for himself on his family's farm? He would have to risk his heart to find out. He only wished he felt even slightly confident in the answer to that question.

Over the next week, he tied up loose ends in Illinois, explaining his sudden change of heart to the elderly Amish man who had leased his farm to Jeremy. The other man understood his decision and wished him well, making arrangements to give Jeremy a portion of the profits from the crops he had so diligently planted.

"Good luck, Jeremy," he said, waving farewell as Jeremy prepared to set off in a van packed full of the possessions he'd accumulated over the past five years.

"*Denki*, Mr. Slauchier," Jeremy replied.

Jeremy had a feeling he was going to need it. And a half dozen appeals to *Gott* wouldn't hurt either. The prayers served to help calm his nerves a bit, at least.

But there were things he needed to do, if he ever hoped to be able to offer Lovina the kind of life she truly deserved. Difficult things he must face before he could ask her to consider sharing a future with him. He wasn't entirely certain he could do what was necessary. However, he refused to come to her burdened by the past. He cared too deeply for her to tie her to him while forgiveness for his *daed* remained just out of reach.

He had a lot of time to think during the trip back to his family farm, and when he reached the farmhouse, he paid the van driver, unloaded his things and immediately set to work cleaning. After the cobwebs and thick layer of dust had been removed and the linens were aired, he spent the rest of the day repairing a broken shutter here and a rotted board there, then he began painting the whole house inside and out, using the numerous cans of white paint he'd discovered in the barn.

It took him a good two weeks, and during that time, he hadn't seen Lovina at all. He'd intentionally kept a low profile, not really wanting anyone to know he was there.

When he finished working on the house, he was surprised by how light it appeared. Not just physically, but in spirit, too. He realized it wasn't just the house that was lighter, it was himself, as well—as though a great weight had been lifted from his shoulders.

Even the clouded memories of his father didn't weigh him down like before. It was almost as if with every swipe of his paint brush and every pound of his hammer, he was cleaning and brightening himself, not just the house. He'd gotten into the habit of praying while he worked, and with his increased closeness to God came an increased feeling of being forgiven and being set free. The bitterness he'd harbored in his heart for so long began to chip away, replaced by a surprising feeling of compassion—both for himself and for his father.

Was he at last, becoming a man worthy of Lovina?

The farmhouse looked exactly as it had before his *mamm* left all those years ago. Although Jeremy's *daed* had always been strict, it had started to get much worse after her leaving. At times, it had seemed as though Isaiah hated his sons. But it couldn't have been easy trying to raise five boys alone.

Had bitterness eaten away at Isaiah in the same way it had almost consumed Jeremy? Until there was nothing left in Isaiah's heart but anger and resentment? But unlike Jeremy, the older man hadn't been able to pull himself free. No one had offered Isaiah any kind of support or compassion—the kind of support Jeremy felt from Lovina, even when they weren't talking directly about it.

Jeremy felt as though he had gained a greater understanding of his *daed*, that he was seeing the older man more clearly than he ever had before. With that realization, forgiving Isaiah became so much more possible. Not exactly easy, but possible.

Jeremy knew for sure and for certain that he didn't want to carry around hatred and resentment. It had already robbed him of enough.

He knew he'd be able to sort through his *daed's* belongings now without the risk that it might push him back to the dark place where he'd been imprisoned for much too long. The memories of the past no longer sent jagged shards of pain through him. He intended to make new memories here now—hopefully, with Lovina.

He could finally admit to himself that he loved Lovina. And he didn't want to wait a moment longer to find out if there was any chance she might feel the same way about him one day.

Chapter Thirteen

Lovina had hoped to receive another letter from Jeremy, but she received something even better when she learned he'd arrived unexpectedly in town. She wouldn't get her hopes up about what his presence might mean, however. He was probably just there to see to the farm. Whatever that might entail, she doubted he planned to be in Indiana for more than a short visit.

Still, she couldn't deny she would be glad to see him.

"Why didn't you tell me you were coming?" she asked him later that day.

"I did write you a letter, but then I figured I would be able to travel faster than the mail, so I brought it with me." He pulled an envelope from the pocket of his dark coat.

He handed it to her as though he expected to stand there staring at her while she read it.

"Why don't you tell me what it says instead?" she suggested.

He hesitated, seeming suddenly tongued-tied and lost for words. She wondered what exactly he had written in the letter to cause such a reaction. Surely, he must have said something a bit more significant than merely mentioning he intended to visit.

Lovina gripped the unopened envelope tightly in her hand causing the paper to crinkle, as she waited for his reply.

Jeremy reached out to take her free hand. Lovina's heart rate picked up speed. She cautioned herself not to leap to any conclusions just yet. She didn't want to start imagining a life with him only to have her hopes dashed yet again—even if she couldn't think of any other logical reason to explain his unexpected behavior on the heels of his surprise return to Baker's Corner.

Jeremy cleared his throat. "I'd like to court you, if you have no objection."

A surprised gasp slipped from her lips. It was more than she'd dared dream of over the past several weeks since he'd left, despite the handful of letters they'd exchanged.

"*Nee*. I mean, *jah*," she answered.

Jeremy's eyebrows pinched together quizzically, and she

realized she wasn't making herself clear. His astonishing announcement left her flustered, and she felt herself blush.

"I'd be pleased to enter into a courtship with you," she clarified, unable to contain her smile of pure happiness.

His mouth curved into a wide grin, but it slipped slightly as she continued.

"Do you intend this to be a long-distance courtship?" That possibility didn't fill her with joy. She didn't want to spend large stretches of time apart. "You must know that I can't leave my parents. And if you're planning to go back to Illinois—"

"I'm not planning to," he asserted, cutting off her protests. "I've decided to move back to my family's farm and make my home there."

"You'll be staying here in Baker's Corner? Forever?" She could hardly believe his words.

He nodded in reply. "Is that's agreeable to you?"

"*Ach*, but it'll be right nice to have you close again," she said with heartfelt conviction.

She reached up to tuck an errant strand of hair behind her ear, and only then did she remember the envelope she still held.

She wondered if Jeremy had put his desire to start a courtship in writing. If so, she intended to tuck the letter away as a special keepsake. Even if there was no mention of courting her, she'd still keep the letter and add it to all the others. Although there was nothing of monumental significance in the collection of letters she'd received from Jeremy up till now, she hadn't wanted to get rid of any of them.

She had tried to convince herself she hadn't fallen in love with him. That he hadn't taken her heart with him. She hadn't wanted to admit the truth after he left, when she believed he'd never return. But the bundle of letters tied with a lavender ribbon belied all her false assertions.

Later that evening, she opened his letter and tears filled her eyes as she read.

Dear Lovina,

I'm coming back to Baker's Corner. I can no longer pretend that I didn't leave my heart there. That I didn't leave my heart with you.

Because I did, you know. I can no longer imagine my life without you. I can no longer live apart from you. I do hope, nee, I pray that you'll accept my courtship. I want us to spend time together, to get to know each other better, to plan our future.

I want a future with you, Lovina. Please say yes. Please agree to let me court you.

Yours,

Jeremy

Jeremy spent as much time with Lovina as he could over the next several weeks, but it didn't feel like nearly enough to suit him. There was no remedy, however, as they both had responsibilities that required their attention. He was often busy tending to his farm, while she had little time to spare after helping out her parents and working at the bakery. Without Ruth's presence, the situation would have been worse, so Jeremy counted his blessings rather than lamenting what couldn't be changed.

But it did get him to thinking about the day when he and Lovina could reside together, and they'd have much more time to share with each other. Although he was eager to propose, he didn't want to rush things.

They had talked about how they envisioned their life together. Lovina would never abandon her parents, and Jeremy would certainly never expect that of her. It did present come challenges, however.

Jeremy wanted to continue to make his home on the farm, and there was enough room at the farmhouse for the older couple to live there with him and Lovina after they were married. Although Lovina was open to the idea, they hadn't come to any firm decision on the subject yet. That would likely take place after their engagement.

If Lovina decided that she preferred to stay at the house in town, then Jeremy would move there with her and drive out to the farm each day to tend to the animals and crops. As long as he was with her, he'd be content.

And he wanted her to be happy, too.

He knew she had concerns for her *daed*. She worried the older man would soon forget her entirely. Jeremy tried to comfort her, but there was no escaping the fact that the day would come. The only uncertainty was when it would come.

Until then, Jeremy was determined to offer her whatever support he could, vowing to always be here for her—no matter that the little he was actually able to do scarcely felt like enough. He couldn't take away the disease, couldn't make Lovina's *daed* whole again.

He felt powerless to do anything but sit by while the older man lost a few more pieces of himself with each day that passed. For Lovina, the feeling must have been one hundred times worse as she was forced to watch her *daed* slip farther and farther away from her.

One evening when Jeremy was visiting, he clasped her hands tightly in his. "This terrible situation will never be okay, Lovina. It will never be easy to accept. Your *daed* will never get better. We both know that."

Her lips trembled and tears shone in her green eyes, but she didn't allow them to fall. "Just having you here makes it a bit easier to bear. I don't know what I'd do without you now."

Jeremy had no intention of ever allowing her to find out. He gathered her into his arms, and she rested her head against his shoulder. They sat that way for a long while.

He would sit like this with her forever if he could. He never wanted to let her go.

Chapter Fourteen

Jeremy reached the house where Lovina lived with her parents and climbed the porch stairs. He took a deep breath as he ran his damp palms down the legs of his trousers, then yanked off his hat and hastily straightened his hair. Squaring his shoulders, he raised his hand to knock.

When Ruth opened the door to him, she offered him a polite greeting, her eyebrows lifted in silent question.

"I've come to talk to Mr. Wyse. Is now a good time?"

"He seems to be having a *gut* day today. The last time I looked in on him, he was reading from his Bible. He's in the sunroom off the kitchen." She moved aside to let Jeremy enter the house, and then closed the door behind him.

His steps echoed on the hardwood floor as he walked down the hallway toward the sunroom at the back of the house.

Ruth parted ways with him to return to whatever task he'd pulled her away from upstairs. Perhaps she was helping Mrs. Wyse, since he hadn't seen the older woman in any of the rooms he'd passed.

Jeremy found Lovina's *daed* reclining in a large, comfortable chair with his stocking-clad feet propped up on a padded footstool. He appeared to be asleep, a Bible lying open in his lap. Jeremy didn't want to disturb him, and he started to back away from the doorway. He pulled to a halt when Mr. Wyse shifted suddenly and opened his eyes. The older man's gaze landed directly on Jeremy. Recognition shone in his eyes, and Jeremy breathed a sigh of relief that he would be able to have a serious conversation with him.

"Mr. Wyse, how are you today?"

"Fine." He closed the Bible, his fingers tapping against the worn cover. "But I suspect you didn't come here to inquire about my health. I believe Lovina's at the bakery just now, if you've come in search of her."

"Actually, I wanted to speak to you."

"Well then, have a seat." The older man waved to a chair, then set his Bible on the glass-topped table at his side. "Now, what's on your mind?" he asked once Jeremy had settled into the indicated seat.

"I'm sure you're aware I've been courting you daughter?" It came out sounding more like a question than a statement, and he worried whether Lovina's *daed* might take offense.

But he didn't show any signs of upset. Instead, the corners of his mouth turned up slightly in amusement. "*Jah,* Lovina has talked of little else recently."

Mr. Wyse's words and affable manner should have served to calm Jeremy, but it didn't ease the tension he felt. He gulped noisily, trying to dislodge the lump that had formed in his throat.

"I-I... well, I know this isn't always customary, but I wanted to ask for your blessing to marry Lovina."

The older man was silent for a long moment, and Jeremy couldn't read anything in his expression. He rubbed his palms against the fabric of his trousers, unable to sit still without fidgeting.

Mr. Wyse shifted in his chair, the wood creaking beneath him as he moved. "I suspected you might be heading in that direction. You have my blessing, if Lovina will have you. But I have a feeling that won't pose a problem."

Jeremy wished he felt as confident as Mr. Wyse did. Although Lovina saying no seemed unlikely given his recent discussions about the future, there was always the chance she would refuse him. But he intended to do everything in his power to see that didn't happen.

He just hoped he didn't do anything to mess it up.

He stood, feeling deeply grateful. "Thank you," he said to the elderly man, who was now looking up at him with a wide grin. "I will do everything I can to make Lovina happy if she says yes."

"I don't doubt that for a minute, young man. I don't doubt that for a minute."

When Lovina exited the bakery that afternoon, she discovered Jeremy waiting for her. A smile instantly spread across her face and joy filled her heart.

"Will you allow me to walk you home?" he asked.

"Of course," she agreed immediately.

He fell into step beside her, but he didn't take her hand in his as had become his custom when they walked together since he'd started courting her. His sudden odd behavior made her feel off balance. Silence stretched out between them. She wanted to reach for his hand, but she interlaced her fingers in front of her instead, stifling the impulse.

Jeremy was unusually quiet during the short walk. He cleared his throat a few times, as though he had something he wanted to say, but no words emerged. He seemed restless and not quite himself.

Lovina started to tell him an amusing story about a child who had come into the bakery that day, but then she thought better of it. Given his current demeanor, the story suddenly didn't seem as humorous as it had earlier.

But the silence left her alone with her thoughts, which were suddenly filled with circling doubts.

Had Jeremy decided to end their courtship, but he didn't know how to tell her? Did he plan to go back to Illinois? He had seemed to be settling into his life here. He'd appeared happy. Or had she been mistaken about that?

She believed that he returned her feelings, that he was coming to love her. Had she been wrong about that, too? Had she misconstrued the situation so badly that she was dreaming of a wedding, while he was trying to figure out a way to extricate himself in order to return to a life without her in it?

By the time they reached her house, he still hadn't spoken, and she couldn't help thinking that she was right in assuming the worst. What other explanation could there be for his unusual silence?

She didn't want to allow Jeremy to see her distress, but she feared it must show on her face. Suddenly, she was anxious to put off this conversation, even though she knew delaying it would make no difference to the outcome. She wasn't strong enough to hear him say the words, however. Not yet. She needed time to prepare herself. Although how could a person prepare for their heart to be shattered? She would never be ready to accept it calmly—no matter how much time she had to come to terms with it.

Feeling an overwhelming urge to escape, she reached for the doorknob.

Jeremy stopped her with a hand on her arm, finding his voice at last. "Wait, Lovina. I have something I want to say to you."

She was desperate to flee. Or to cover her ears so she didn't have to listen. His hold on her prevented that, however. She might have been able to take him by surprise and break free to make her escape, but it would be useless in the end. She could not avoid this forever.

Best to get it over with quickly then.

Nonetheless, it was with no small amount of reluctance that she turned back to face him. Forcing her gaze to meet his, she lifted her chin. She would not weep or plead with him. Only when she was alone in her room would she allow the tears to fall.

"You want to end our courtship, don't you?" She blurted out the words, imagining that her saying them might somehow make it hurt less.

But it didn't help. Not even a little bit. Stabbing the knife in herself hadn't made it any easier for her to bear the pain. She felt completely gutted. It had been extremely foolish of her to believe otherwise.

An expression crossed Jeremy's face she couldn't quite read, and he nodded his head in answer to her question. "*Jah.* I believe it's time. I'd hoped you would agree."

Her head jerked up and down in reaction, though agreement was far from what she felt right now. But a relationship required two willing people, and Jeremy plainly didn't want the same thing she did.

The stiffness left Jeremy's tense frame, as though he were relieved she understood and had taken the burden off him.

Having her worst fears confirmed, the hurt was so sharp that it stole her breath. It was made worse by the fact that she'd had no inkling Jeremy was experiencing doubts. She thought they shared the same vision for the future. A future together. She was taken complete unaware now that he'd revealed his true feelings.

Somehow, she forced herself to speak. "There's no sense in dragging out a courtship when the couple realizes they aren't right for each other. If you believe we don't suit, then—" She gulped in air, struggling to continue. "Then, I—" She tried to get more words out, to say the words that would release him, but it was no use.

"*What?*" Jeremy gasped out, his eyes widening in alarm.

Lovina blinked in confusion, feeling even more off kilter than she had before, though she hadn't believed it possible.

"*That's* what you thought I meant?" He shook his head sharply.

"Lovina, *nee*. I didn't mean that." He laid a hand against her cheek, preventing her from looking away.

Not that she wanted to. Not if she'd jumped to a completely false conclusion, as it was starting to become clear to her that she might have. *Please, Gott,* she prayed fervently. *Let me have been wrong.*

Jeremy met her gaze squarely, sincerity and tenderness shining in his eyes. "I love you, Lovina. I want to marry you. When I said I wanted to end our courtship, I meant that we wouldn't be a courting couple much longer because I hoped you'd consent to be my wife. How could you ever think otherwise?" His features contorted as an expression of pain flashed across his face.

"But you were acting oddly. And you didn't say even one word to me during the entire walk home. I thought—" She cut herself off, her cheeks heating at the memory of her unreasonable panic. "Well, you know what I thought."

"I'm sorry I caused you to think that for even a single moment. And all because I was reluctant to risk possible rejection." He gave her a sheepish smile before his expression sobered once more. "I'm sorry. I was afraid to risk giving you my heart because I feared you might refuse it. But my fear ended up hurting you instead, and that's the last thing I ever wanted to happen. Can you forgive me?"

"Of course," she agreed without hesitation as a wave of relief rushed through her.

She couldn't believe she'd been so silly to panic like that. But she could empathize with how Jeremy had been feeling—believing things were good between them and hoping for a permanent commitment, but unsure of her, uncertain of whether she shared his yearning. After all, wasn't that exactly how she'd felt just moments ago? Wasn't that what had led to their misunderstanding?

Her teeth sank into her bottom lip. "I didn't know you loved me. You'd never said it before."

"Neither did you. You still haven't," he pointed out.

She smiled widely at that. "I love you, Jeremy. And I'll tell you 'I love you' every day for the rest of my life."

A hopeful smile appeared on Jeremy's face. "Does that mean you'll marry me?"

She nodded. "I will."

His eyes lit up as his smile stretched wider. "*Gut.*"

Jah, it was very *gut.*

And it was even better when he pulled her close for a sweet kiss. Her heart flooded with happiness.

When he had first returned to Baker's Corner so many months ago, she hadn't dared to hope they would end up here. She had expected to remain alone, caring for her parents, maybe for the rest of her life. But *Gott* plainly had other plans for her.

She would still care for her parents, but now she'd be doing it with Jeremy by her side, helping her. It wouldn't be a one-sided exchange, however. She was looking forward to making his family farm *their* family farm, just as they had talked about, and moving her parents into the farmhouse. Settling into a life with Jeremy—and filling their home with love.

Maybe they would even be able to convince all of Jeremy's brothers to come back to the farm for a visit during the holidays. Suddenly, anything seemed possible.

She knew there would be trials, but they'd face them together. Jeremy would lend her his strength when she needed it, and she'd do the same for him—the way she'd always imagined it as a young girl when she was dreaming of the life she wanted to share with Jeremy.

Only this was so much better...

Because it was real.

The End

Continue Reading...

Thank you for reading **Sweet Forgiveness! Are you wondering what to read next?** Why not read **Amish Rose? Here's a peek for you:**

Ivy Guth sighed as she hung the new curtains she had just finished sewing. She stood back to scrutinize her handiwork.

"They're lovely," *Aenti* Ruth said, entering the room. "I do love white lace curtains. There's something about them that reminds me of a blank canvas – like there's space for something exciting to take place. Not that fresh new curtains are bland in themselves – they're beautiful, yet have potential for more...if you know what I mean."

"*Aenti* Ruth," Ivy said with a smile, "somehow I don't think you're talking about the curtains right now."

It was Ruth's turn to smile. "Well, look at us – you and me. We have beautiful 'white curtain' lives, but there's a lot of room for something more exciting to happen.

"Hmm…" Ivy murmured, contemplating her aunt's words. Mighty odd words, too, in Ivy's opinion. "Is there something you're thinking of that could make your life more exciting?"

Ruth turned a delicate shade of pink. Ivy wondered whether she was thinking of Deacon Eli, and the way he smiled at her whenever they ran into each other at the local mercantile.

"Well," Ruth said in her matter of fact manner. "You know I can never hope for anything *truly* exciting to happen to me… and it's not just because I've decided to remain single all my life."

"You keep saying that, but I think there are a lot of eligible bachelors around who are not oblivious to the charms of a very attractive, *Gott*-fearing, *gut* woman such as yourself. Not to mention that you're a great cook." Ivy purposely didn't mention Deacon Eli. In truth, she had no idea whether her aunt was interested in him or not. She certainly didn't appear to be interested.

"Oh, come now, Ivy," Ruth protested. "You're beginning to sound like your *mamm*. In fact, she talks of marriage to me so often, I'm beginning to wonder if she and your *daed* are getting tired of having me live here."

"We love having you live here," Ivy replied. "But like me, *Mamm* and *Daed* want you to be happy."

"Enough about me," Ruth countered. "What about you?"

"What about me? I'm doing fine."

"You haven't yet been courted, and you didn't even really take a *Rumspringa*," Ruth remarked. "I feel like you are cheating yourself somehow. You're a lovely girl. And very capable. Why don't you consider accepting the courtship of some nice young boy?"

VISIT HERE To Read More:

http://www.ticahousepublishing.com/amish-miller.html

Thank you for Reading

If you **love Amish Romance, Visit Here:**

https://amish.subscribemenow.com/

to find out about all **New Hannah Miller Amish Romance Releases! We will let you know as soon as they become available!**

If you enjoyed ***Sweet Forgiveness!*** would you kindly take a couple minutes to leave a positive review on Amazon? It only takes a moment, and positive reviews truly make a difference. I would be so grateful! Thank you!

Turn the page to discover more Hannah Miller Amish Romances just for you!

More Amish Romance from Hannah Miller

Visit HERE for Hannah Miller's Amish Romance

https://ticahousepublishing.com/amish-miller.html

About the Author

Hannah Miller has been writing Amish Romance for the past seven years. Long intrigued by the Amish way of life, Hannah has traveled the United States, visiting different Amish communities. She treasures her Amish friends and enjoys visiting with them. Hannah makes her home in Indiana, along with her husband, Robert. Together, they have three children and seven grandchildren. Hannah loves to ride bikes in the sunshine. And if it's warm enough for a picnic, you'll find her under the nearest tree!

Made in the USA
Monee, IL
08 December 2019